Written and illustrated by
Beverley Gooding

This book is dedicated
to Mr. David Rae

This edition published by
Parragon Books Ltd in 2015
and distributed by

Parragon Inc.
440 Park Avenue South, 13th Floor
New York, NY 10016
www.parragon.com

ISBN 978-1-4748-3095-9

Printed in China

Max
and
Tallulah

a little love story

PaRRagon

Bath · New York · Cologne · Melbourne · Delhi
Hong Kong · Shenzhen · Singapore · Amsterdam

Max loved Tallulah

with all his heart.

But he was too shy to tell her.

Max needed a way to make Tallulah notice him. So he decided to give her a present. He picked her favorite fruit, balanced it on a lily leaf, and pushed it carefully along the river.

But just before Max reached Tallulah, the leaf started to sink! All of the fruit fell into the water and floated away.

Max needed another plan.

That night, by the light
of the moon, Max practiced
a daring dance!

When the sun began
to rise, he went to
find Tallulah.

Tallulah was in the forest
looking for juicy leaves.

Max was certain that his daring dance would get her attention.

He stepped forward ...

He tapped his hoof ...

He leapt into the sky ...

And he twirled,
faster and faster!

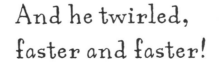

Surely Tallulah would notice him now?

But Tallulah was so busy eating
that she didn't see Max or any
of his daring dance.

Max needed a new idea.

He gathered leaves and flowers and insects of every size and color.

Max was going to make the most magnificent hat Tallulah had ever seen!

Surely that would impress her?

But when Max appeared in his magnificent hat ...

... Tallulah was so startled that she ran away!

Max had not meant to frighten Tallulah.
What could he do now?

Suddenly, Max saw his reflection
in the water, and he had the

greatest idea of all!

He was going to be ...

JUST MAX!

Max smiled at Tallulah ...

... and Tallulah smiled back!

Tallulah and Max walked side by side, and
Max told her all about fruit on lily leaves, a
daring dance, his magnificent hat ... and being
just Max!